Coral and the *Pearl Diver*

Harper Festival is an imprint of HarperCollins Publishers.

Bella Sara #9: Coral and the Pearl Diver
Cover and interior illustrations by Jennifer L. Meyer
For information address HarperCollins Children's Books,
a division of HarperCollins Publishers,
10 East 53rd Street, New York, NY 10022.
www.harpercollinschildrens.com
www.bellasara.com

Library of Congress catalog card number: 2009925073
ISBN 978-0-06-168788-4
09 10 11 12 13   CG/CW   10 9 8 7 6 5 4 3 2 1
❖
First Edition

9

Coral and the Pearl Diver

Written by Felicity Brown
Illustrated by Jennifer L. Meyer

HARPER FESTIVAL
An Imprint of HarperCollinsPublishers

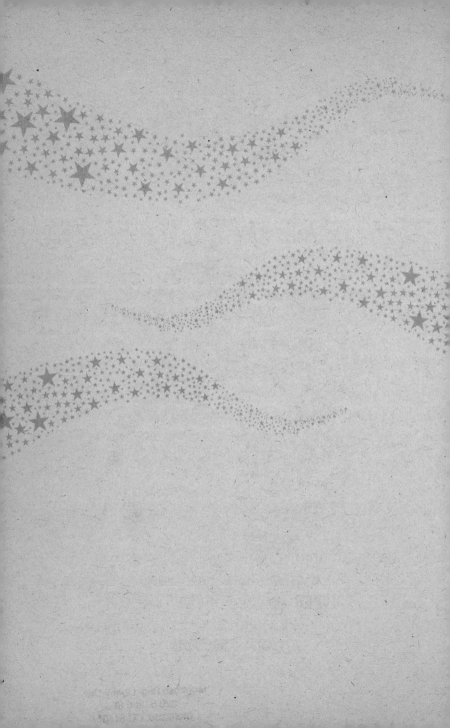

Twelve-year-old Miki Vann adored everything about her native home, the tropical island of Awdi Salaca. But her absolutely favorite thing was the school of lively green water horses who lived in the sea around nearby Bahura Reef.

After an unsuccessful day of diving for luna pearls with her family, Miki was hanging out with the other island children in the late-afternoon sun. Later that night, they would celebrate the biggest festival of the year. Miki sat beside her best friend, Lealoni, on Silver Rock, a huge, shiny stone ledge that hung sixty feet above the aquamarine ocean.

Silver Rock was the best spot on Awdi Salaca to watch the water horses frolicking in the surf. Too bad the horses kept their distance from humans . . . Miki longed to play with them and get to know them better.

Lealoni pointed to a water horse. "It's the red one!" she squealed. "I told you I saw her this morning. There she is! See?"

"I see her," Miki replied, smiling at her friend's excitement. Lealoni was only eight, and some of the other kids teased Miki for hanging around with a girl younger than herself. But Miki loved Lealoni's constant enthusiasm.

Miki and Lealoni watched as the red filly launched herself out of the water in a beautiful breach. The water horse spun and twisted in the sky before slipping back into the sea with the smallest of splashes. As a practiced diver herself, Miki was impressed with the filly's athletic technique.

Lealoni sighed happily, toying with a tiny luna pearl that hung from a cord around her neck. "I bet I could twist just like that if I dived off this cliff," she said.

"You wish!" said someone from behind them. Miki glanced back and saw that it was fifteen-year-old Shad, surrounded by a group of younger boys. Shad looked muscular and tough, but Miki had known him her whole life and knew he was more sensitive than he seemed.

"Shrimp, you'd be squashed like a jellyfish on the rocks," Shad mocked Lealoni. The boys around Shad laughed.

Miki glared at Shad. "You're just a *jumbo* shrimp," she told him. "You can't dive from this high, either."

"And you can?" Shad challenged. "Go on then, I dare you!"

Miki considered the dare. She felt

a little scared, even though she was confident in her diving abilities. Silver Rock was the highest point on Awdi Salaca's coast. It would be easy to get injured.

"Of course Miki can dive from here!" Lealoni piped up. "She's the best diver on the island!"

Miki shot a pained glance at Lealoni. It was great that her friend was so loyal, but now Miki would look like a wimp if she didn't take up the challenge.

"So, prove it," Shad said to Miki with a shrug.

With a deep breath, Miki stood up. "No problem," she said, and all the kids cheered.

Miki stepped closer to the edge. She peered down at the swirling blue-green water far below. She wasn't afraid of heights. The water was deep in the bay below Silver Rock, so there was no chance of being hurt by hitting the bottom. She'd seen adults dive from this location many times. But still—diving from this height, she'd hit the water *hard*. It would take all her skill to pierce the surface of the water safely.

Letting herself relax, Miki stared across the water at the spectacular scenery of Awdi Salaca. The island was a tropical paradise. It was roughly butterfly-shaped, with a cove cutting into both the north and south sides. The cliffs along the shoreline were broken by sloping pinkish or black sand beaches, along with the occasional waterfall. Tall, solitary rock formations called sea stacks jutted from the surf. Awdi Salaca was forested by bluish palms and tangled jungle vines, speckled with giant red and yellow flowers.

In the center, looming over all the natural beauty, was Mount Salaca, the active volcano that had created it all. Smoke wisped out of the caldera, the hot mouth at the peak of the volcano.

Miki concentrated on her dive, focusing on the spot in the sea she planned to hit. A tremor of fear churned in her stomach, but then the red filly breached again at the edge of Miki's vision. Seeing the water horse leap so gracefully gave Miki the courage to launch herself off the cliff.

She soared out from Silver Rock. For a long moment she felt as though she were hanging motionless in the sky, defying gravity like a winged horse.

But then gravity yanked her toward the ocean. Her long hair whipped in the rushing wind as she plummeted.

Miki tucked her legs, rolling into a neat somersault. Then she extended her body, twisting it like the whorls of a conch shell. Before she hit the water, she arched her back, making sure her legs were straight behind her and her hands were splayed wide in front of either side of her head.

Her hands smacked the ocean, breaking the hard surface of the water and creating a hole for her head. The entry was smooth—she knew she'd barely left a splash.

As she arced underwater, Miki's whole body tingled in excitement. A dive from that high was such a rush!

Now she could feel the sting on her hands, the sides of her arms, and the tops of her feet where the water had slapped. She settled underwater and let her smarting skin cool. Miki could hold her breath a long time—a skill she'd learned from diving for pearls almost before she could walk. As always, the silence underwater filled her with a sense of deep peace.

Wriggling multicolored fish darted by, weaving between tangles of seaweed growing on the sides of the cliff. An unusual type of eel Miki had never seen before—with yellow and blue shimmering scales and flamboyant fins—twisted around a sunken boulder. The eel streaked away as a star-shaped sea stelly tried to zap it with electricity. Miki tracked the glimmering trail of the eel as it shot into the distance toward the wavering shadow of Bahura Reef, where a wonderland of more magical undersea marvels awaited.

Miki's chest tightened as her air began running out. She glanced toward the surface, ready to head up.

Before she could move, the red water horse swam into view.

Both Miki and the water horse remained still, staring at each other. Miki could see now that the filly's color wasn't true red—she had dark pink scales with scarlet and white highlights. Her color was closer to the gorgeous shade of the fire coral that grew on Bahura Reef. Her head resembled a noble land horse's, although she had a long, thick, red mane that looked more like silky sea fronds than hair. The filly's forelegs were muscular, with delicate webbing from her knees to her fetlocks, the tufts of hair just above her hooves. Her glossy body tapered down to a wide flipper tail.

The water horse's nostrils flared, bubbles trailing out as she whinnied silently. She seemed as interested in inspecting Miki as Miki was fascinated by her.

Miki's heart beat faster as the water horse swam closer. She floated gently as the filly came near enough to touch.

The water horse had the most beautiful dark eyes Miki had ever seen, and she couldn't help smiling when the filly blinked her big eyelashes.

Miki slowly raised her hand to brush the water horse's nose, which felt surprisingly warm, soft, and sleek. Miki's heart ached, flooded with overwhelming tenderness toward the beautiful filly. And the strain of breathlessness in her lungs eased—

Splash!

The water horse shied away as something heavy landed in the water nearby.

Miki spotted a boy's legs flailing,

and she recognized Shad as he shot by feetfirst. Shad had been too much of a jellyfish to dive, so he'd jumped. His stomach and legs were bright red from where he'd hit the water.

The filly gave Miki a final glance before zooming away. She had disappeared behind the reef before Shad's bubbles cleared.

Miki's lungs felt tight again. She kicked her legs, shooting up toward the surface. When she reached air, she gasped for breath. Then she couldn't help laughing loudly, feeling giddy from the encounter with the water horse.

When Shad surfaced, Miki splashed him. "You should always wait until the first diver is out of the water!" she scolded.

Shad just grinned back, thrilled by his first big jump.

Miki shook her head at him, and then swam beside him toward the shore.

The water changed color as they

reached the beach, reflecting the pastel sunset in an amazing coral hue, the same shade as the water horse.

Miki's feet trembled as she waded out of the water onto the sand. At first, she thought it was just the excitement of her successful dive, or the thrill of meeting the amazing water horse.

But no—it was Mount Salaca waking up.

In the center of the island, the volcano rumbled again and spewed out smoke into the darkening sky.

2

*M*iki said good-bye to Lealoni at the base of the slope that led up to Silver Rock. Their homes were on different sides of the island. Miki lived on the windward half of Awdi Salaca, which got a lot more rain than the dry, western side. The towering volcano blocked storm clouds from crossing from east to west.

The rumbles of Mount Salaca were growing more intense. Miki rushed along the damp path through the rain forest until she reached her family's house. The wooden structure, built by her father, was set up on stilts.

"You're late!" Miki's mother complained when she heard Miki on the front stairs. "Get dressed quickly now."

Miki hurried to change out of her everyday sarong into the traditional muumuu patterned with blue flowers that all young women wore to the Festival of Volcanic Light. The festival celebrated the volcano's annual eruption at the approach of spring. Every year the islanders performed a ritual in the hope of increasing the undersea life on the reef. The people of Awdi Salaca depended on fishing and harvesting sea creatures for their survival.

When Miki finished dressing, she called out to her mother. "Will you help me with my hair?" she asked.

"One day you'll do this for your own daughter," her mother said, as she began to weave tea leaves and coral beads into Miki's hair in a complex pattern.

The house seemed unusually quiet.

"Where's Vegar?" Miki asked.

"He's already gone ahead," Miki's mother replied, a note of pride in her voice. Miki's brother, Vegar, had been chosen as a Light Bearer in the ritual. It was a great honor. "And your father's at the beach, setting up his display."

Miki could feel the vibrations of the volcano through the house's floorboards. She fidgeted while her mother finished braiding her hair.

Miki couldn't wait for the festivities. It was such an exciting celebration, with feasting and dancing under the Auroborus lights. But her favorite part was the running of the volcano's lava horses. It was thrilling to watch the horses run into the ocean, bringing forth the brilliant fire spoops, fish that fertilize the reef annually. If the fire spoops stayed by the reef, it meant the island would thrive.

Although the fire spoops had always stayed in Miki's lifetime, last year there had been only a few. So the fishing harvest had been weak. It was crucial this year that the running of the lava horses awakened more fire spoops so Awdi Salaca would return to its past prosperity.

The sun had set by the time Miki and her mother arrived at the festival. The two moons, the giant ringed planet, and the Auroborus lights were already shimmering in the night sky.

Lealoni met Miki at the pass in the dunes that led down to Broad Beach. Torches flickered along the pass and on the beach below. Broad Beach was protected by two cliffs that rose jaggedly on either side.

Miki's mother greeted Lealoni's parents and then headed off to find her own friends. "Say hello to your father for me," her mother instructed Miki. "And don't be late meeting us at Four Palms to watch the ritual."

As soon as the adults were gone,

Miki and Lealoni turned toward each other, letting out squeals of excitement.

"Let's go see the pearl displays," said Lealoni. "Or the spear fisher contest. Or the cliff-climbing race. Or the squidling wrestling."

"Food first," Miki said.

With the delicious scents wafting from across the beach, Lealoni couldn't argue. They stopped at booths and fire pits, sampling fish baked with cinnamon sticks, sticks of crab meat wrapped in dough and fried, and candy made from the sap of a sweet mountain shrub.

When the girls were full, they crossed the crowded beach to visit Miki's father at his luna pearl display. Miki's family was descended from a long line of famous pearl divers. Each diver family set up a booth that showed off their most famous pearls from generations past, as well as their best find of the year. The medium and small pearls were sold to buyers all around North of North, but the biggest ones were kept as a historical record.

At Miki's father's booth, she was shocked to see how the luna pearls had shrunk over the past years. The biggest one this year was barely half the size of the best from twenty years ago, and that one was half the size of ten years before that.

"Why are the pearls so small now?" Miki asked her father.

Her father tried to smile reassuringly, but he looked worried. "The fire spoops will come tonight," he said, "and get those lazy oysters working harder next year, hmm?"

Miki laughed, even though he had evaded her question. She hoped he was right. She had found only four little pearls in the past year, her worst crop since she'd started to dive. Miki knew the family's pearls this year would barely support them for the coming season. "Maybe one of the oysters this year will make a new Heart of the Sea," she joked.

Mr. Vann shook his head. "There is only one Heart of the Sea," he said solemnly. "Our ancestors gifted it to the water horses to protect Celestial Deep, their undersea kingdom."

Miki smiled at her father. He knew the story of the Heart of the Sea was her favorite legend.

The beach trembled under Miki's feet as Mount Salaca growled. The smoke issuing from the volcano darkened and thickened. The islanders cheered the rumbling, and the music for dancing started up.

Lealoni grabbed Miki's hand and pulled her over to watch the dancers. Islanders of all ages wriggled and shimmied on the beach, bopping to the beat of the music. Shad, ten-year-old twin boys named Kei and Wilai, and a girl Miki's age named Peloni surrounded Miki and Lealoni, pushing them into the dance.

"Recovered from your belly flop yet?" Miki teased Shad, as she danced beside him.

Shad's face reddened. "It didn't hurt," he insisted, but then he smiled. "Okay, my stomach still stings a little bit."

"My hands do, too," Miki admitted. "I can't believe I dived from Silver Rock!"

"I can't believe I jumped!" Shad said.

Then the music shifted into Miki's favorite tune, and she got lost in dancing to the song the musicians played on their conch shells, reed flutes, and big barrel drums. Tremors from the volcano rumbled more frequently under her feet.

When the song ended, a hush fell over the crowd. The Light Bearers proceeded up the sides of the cliffs on specially cut walkways, solemnly carrying their torches as the drums thumped and the volcanic tremors increased in intensity. Miki got goose bumps as Mount Salaca let out a deafening belch of thick smoke.

For centuries, the volcano had erupted like clockwork every year on the same day as the lava horses made their run to the sea.

Miki and Lealoni found their parents, who were standing close together by four palm trees in the middle of the shoreline.

"There's Vegar," Miki's mother whispered, nodding her head toward the torch bearers on the cliff to their right. Miki had already spotted her older brother and felt a pang of jealousy at the honor he had been given. She could dive as well as he could! Someday she would be a Light Bearer, too.

The volcano thundered violently, and the entire population of the island fell silent. Miki joined everyone in turning to look at the top of Mount Salaca just as the volcano spewed up a fiery blast of brilliant orange magma and smoke.

The islanders started to chant a wordless song reserved for this festival. Miki joined in with the women's part, a high wail that was a cross between a cheer of joy and a terrified cry. All the islanders grabbed the hands of the people standing beside them. Miki grasped her father's calloused hand and the trembling soft hand of Lealoni.

Miki felt Lealoni flinch as two blazing meteors shot out of the caldera, soaring skyward, trailing tails of lava. Miki hoped the lava horses would fly directly overhead so she could see them in all their glory.

The two meteors circled the volcano once, zooming beside each other across the smoky sky.

"Awdi!" the islanders chanted. "Salaca!" They called the lava horses by their names, coaxing them to fly to the reef, "Awdi! Salaca! *Awdi, Salaca!*"

The lava horses flew lower, close

enough for Miki to see Awdi's molten body glowing against the starlit night, and his mate Salaca's legs, galloping through the smoke.

Miki turned around with the rest of the islanders to watch the Light Bearers dive off the cliffs. Their torches seemed to hang in the sky as they leaped, creating a path for the lava horses to follow toward the reef.

Seconds after the Light Bearers entered the ocean, the lava horses hit the water with a sizzling splash. The Light Bearers let go of their torches, which sank to the ocean bottom still brightly lit. Their flames burned at a special waterproof pitch that would keep them alight for a few minutes.

The water between the beach and the reef churned in a bubbling hot froth and then settled to a glassy calm. The sea glowed with shimmering blue and green lights as the heat of the lava horses activated the phosphorescent plankton that

lived around the island.

Miki's father squeezed her hand as the islanders fell silent again, scanning the ocean hopefully. The shining plankton were supposed to coax the fire spoops up from their hidden lava tunnels under the ocean bed. Then the fire spoops would fertilize the reef for the coming year.

Silently they waited, searching for a sign of the fire spoops' appearance.

"There!" Lealoni shouted, pointing at the water.

Miki strained to see where her friend was pointing. Then she saw a reddish orange tinge to the waves over the reef. The color was coming from below the water, as the glowing fire spoops rose from the depths.

Mr. Vann let out a long sigh of relief as the water grew redder, with deeper streaks of orange light shimmering across the surface.

The islanders cheered as the fire spoops swarmed around the reef, glowing with the intense colors of an underwater inferno.

Miki clapped and whistled, thrilled that the fire spoops had returned. The past year had been so bad for fishing, and the lean time had affected every aspect of life on the island. A full fertilization by the fire spoops would ensure a prosperous and happy year on Awdi Salaca. . . .

The reddish orange glow abruptly faded.

A worried hush fell over the crowd.

Everyone shuffled nervously on the beach as the light dimmed further, waning quickly now as the fire spoops retreated to their tunnels.

This can't be happening, Miki thought, covering her mouth with her hand in horror. *The fire spoops must stay! They must.*

But moments later, the only illumination on the ocean was the faint reflection of the distant lights in the night sky.

3

*S*tunned by the devastating turn of events, the islanders murmured worriedly. A few sobs could be heard as people huddled together, shuffling toward their homes.

Miki's father let go of her hand to comfort her mother. Together the three of them wandered back to the rainforest side of the island. On the way, Miki listened to her father worry about Awdi Salaca's future.

Without fish, food would be scarce. The native fruits and vegetables wouldn't provide enough nourishment for the islanders. Miki's father explained that there was no money to buy food from the other islands or the mainland, especially since the luna pearls had been so sparse. The people of Awdi Salaca were facing hunger, maybe even starvation.

Exhausted and disappointed, Miki went to bed soon after arriving home. She swung sleepless in her hammock for a while, listening to her parents' low, frightened voices coming from their room.

Miki sat up when Vegar stomped up the stairs. "We did everything right!" he blurted out angrily. "We followed every tradition! So why have the fire spoops forsaken us?"

"Stay calm," Mr. Vann said. "It's not our place to question why the natural world swings from one season to another. We must hold fast to tradition and wait out the changes."

Miki heard her brother groan

in frustration. "Just wait while we all starve?"

"Hush, both of you," Mrs. Vann hissed. "Nothing we do tonight will change anything. We're all upset, and we should all go to sleep now. We'll make a plan when a new day dawns tomorrow."

Miki tossed and turned, wondering what she could do to help. It was a long time before she fell asleep.

In the morning, Miki met up with the other island children on Broad Beach to help with the daily chores. Their duties included cleaning and repairing the fishing nets and pearl-diving tubs. Miki sat on a piece of driftwood between Lealoni and Shad and began scraping barnacles off a bucket. It felt so pointless to be preparing the fishing equipment when there would be no fish.

"We need more luna pearls," Peloni whined. She tied her long blond hair back with a piece of string. "I don't understand why the fire spoops didn't stay."

"I think . . . my father said . . . the reef is dying," Shad replied.

Miki was going to protest, but ducked her head as she thought of something. "Remember when the reef used to light up?" she asked. "The whole reef used to be bright as a full moon when I went pearl diving with my parents at night." She swallowed, remembering that happier time. "Now the reef is dim."

"My mother said something is scaring away—" Kei began.

"The fire spoops," Wilai finished. The twins often completed each other's sentences.

"But what?" asked Lealoni. She shook out the small net she was untangling.

"Shiver sharks, I think," Shad answered. "They even come into the bay now. I saw some fins over by Silver Rock yesterday."

The children all shuddered. There was nothing they feared more than shiver sharks in the water.

"We need to do something to help our families," Miki said. "At least until the fish return."

"What?" Peloni shot back. "We can't make the fish come back!"

"No," Miki said, "but we can dive for pearls. If we gather enough pearls, we can buy food from other islands."

"I'll help!" Lealoni offered eagerly. She jiggled the tiny pearl that hung around her neck. "I found this last summer."

"That pearl is tiny," Peloni scoffed. "We couldn't buy a sandwich with that speck."

"But I did find it," said Lealoni, returning to the knots in her net.

Miki had an idea, but it seemed a little crazy, even to her. "We could swim out to Hazard Point," she suggested. "Nobody's gone diving there in years."

"Hazard Point!" Peloni screeched. "Has the sun baked your brain? There's a reason why they call it Hazard Point. Count me out."

"I guess we can count you out of everything," retorted Kei. "You never have any ideas—"

"Just complaints and insults," Wilai finished.

"There are shiver sharks everywhere at Hazard Point," Shad reminded Miki. "Plus the current there is really strong . . . and it washes out to sea. We can't dive there."

Miki sighed. "I know," she said, "but I can't think of any other options. There are no more mature oysters nearby. There are only baby oyster spats by the beach—nothing old enough to make a pearl. Hazard Point is the only spot we haven't searched."

"So are we going?" Lealoni asked.

Peloni groaned in frustration. "Forget about Hazard Point!" she cried. "It's just too dangerous."

Miki let the subject drop from the

conversation, but not from her mind.

That night, she had an amazing dream. She was swimming through a vast undersea kingdom. She coasted past towering coral cathedrals and stone monuments, all teeming with fish of every imaginable color. Then the coral-colored water horse was there, swimming beside her. She led Miki to a beautiful oyster . . . and inside, Miki knew, was a golden pearl. It gleamed from between the gaps in the oyster's shell.

Miki rose early, feeling recharged by her dream. She decided to sneak out and go pearl diving—at Hazard Point! It was a rule that divers were not allowed to go out alone, but Miki couldn't risk putting any of the other children in so much danger. She shuddered to think what might happen to Lealoni at Hazard Point!

Miki paddled her canoe around the island until she came to the tip of Hazard Point. It was a narrow jut of land—the tail of Awdi Salaca's butterfly—where the waters coursed between the reef and the island into the open ocean.

The early-morning sun was on the far side of the island, backlighting Mount Salaca in faerie fire as Miki launched her canoe into the powerful current. She paddled over to a tall sea stack towering out of the sea.

Miki had borrowed her father's prized spider-silk rope. It had been passed down in the Vann family for generations. Fully extended, the rope stretched to almost one hundred times Miki's body length. She tied one end of the coiled rope to a sturdy rock on the sea stack and the other end around her waist. If the current got too strong, she could pull herself back. The spider silk was almost impossible to break and could easily hold her weight.

Then Miki set up an oyster tub in a tide pool on the sea stack. Even if she didn't find any pearls, there was no reason to waste the oyster meat.

Miki knew it was unlikely that she'd find a golden pearl, but finding a decent-sized luna pearl would be reward enough.

With a deep breath, Miki dived into the current. She was an excellent swimmer—even Shad and Vegar had a hard time keeping up with her—but the current was frighteningly strong.

The rope will protect me, Miki reminded herself. It was thin but sturdy. *I'll be fine.*

Down she swam through the turbulent water, toward the base of Bahura Reef. The reef was only twenty feet away from the sea stack, but the channel was deep . . . and dark. A school of odd, chunky, big-eyed sea creatures called finlings helped light Miki's way by flashing the luminescent lights attached to their heads as they hunted along the reef in the murky water. Timid sea anemones ducked inside the reef's crevasses as Miki approached.

When Miki got closer to the reef, the coral palisade protected her from the current. She was surprised at how easy it was to swim there—the water was fast, but not impossibly rapid.

Wary of brushing against the sharp coral, Miki began her search for oysters. She saw a luna oyster straight-away and spotted two others nearby. Miki felt a glimmer of hope that coming to Hazard Point had been a good idea after all.

After pulling the big luna oyster from its bed, Miki pried it open with her knife. Immediately she saw a silver glow—a luna pearl was inside! She lifted the pearl free from the shell. The jewel was big, perfectly formed, and glowed brightly in her hand. She smiled, feeling a thrill of exhilaration at her find.

With the pearl safely secured in a pouch at her waist, Miki carried the oyster up to the surface. It was always better to be safe and not stay under for too

long, or the gasses in her body would bubble as she rose and she would suffer from painful diver's cramps. When she reached the air, she pulled herself along the rope back to the sea stack.

Miki put the oyster in the tub and then got ready for her next dive.

The second dive was harder. The current had kicked up, and it took longer to reach the reef. When Miki got there, she was surprised by how dark it was. Where had the bright finlings gone?

Feeling nervous, Miki swam to the spot where she'd seen the second oyster. She had just picked it up off its bed when a dark shadow loomed over her.

The rope jerked abruptly as Miki was yanked away from the reef.

After flailing in the water, she managed to right herself. She saw that a hulking shiver shark had gotten its tail tangled in the spider-silk rope.

Cold fear clenched Miki's whole body. Silver lights rippled along the shark's flanks, making it look as if it were trembling. Shiver sharks flashed their lights only when they were enraged or when they had prey in their sights.

The shark thrashed against the bindings, and Miki was whipped around like a rag doll. The shiver shark gnashed the rope with its teeth, but couldn't bite through. And Miki had made sure that she was securely fastened to it!

Now she fumbled at the knot she'd tied. It was too tight and wouldn't loosen. Miki desperately tried to roll the rope off her waist, but the panicked shark's flailing made it impossible.

Soon she would be out of air.

With a violent lurch, the shiver shark pulled the rope toward the open ocean. The spider silk stretched so far that Miki couldn't make out the sea stack or the reef, down in the depths of dark water.

Struggling wildly, the shiver shark finally freed its tail from the rope. After circling twice, the shark turned to face Miki. Silver lights gleamed down its sides.

She stared into its flat, black eyes as it sailed toward her. Its savage maw opened wide.

Miki squeezed her eyes shut and waited for the end.

It didn't come.

Instead, she felt a sudden rush of current around her. Miki opened her eyes. The water in front of her was whirling with colorful commotion.

The shiver shark had forgotten about her. It was busy fending off the front hooves of a kicking water horse— the beautiful coral-colored filly.

She had come to Miki's rescue!

The water horse and shiver shark

sparred in a dangerous dance. The water horse was quicker and more agile, darting away from the shark's thrusts and snapping teeth. The filly boxed the shark squarely on the nose with a hard front hoof.

Miki's lungs were burning—she needed air. She could hold her breath longer than most humans, but she was almost out of oxygen. Glancing up, she couldn't even see the surface, and, for a dizzying moment, she thought she was upside down.

A glimmering blue and yellow eel wriggled over to Miki and stuck the tip of its tail into the spider-silk knot around Miki's waist, instantly loosening it. Then the eel wrapped its whole body around her hand and yanked her up with surprising speed toward the surface.

The shark had dragged Miki deeper than she'd ever been before. She wasn't sure she was going to make it, even with the mysterious eel pulling

her up so rapidly.

At last Miki breached the surface, gasping in deep gulps. The air tasted very sweet. The coral water horse swam up to meet her.

The horse turned her neck and met Miki's eyes. A quick image appeared in Miki's mind—sitting on the water horse with her arms clasped tightly around the filly's neck. The image had come from the water horse! Gasping in amazement, Miki immediately followed orders.

As soon as Miki was securely mounted, the water horse pumped her muscular tail fin, propelling them through the aquamarine waters.

When the filly had carried Miki far enough away from the reef to be safe, the horse launched herself out of the water. Together Miki and the filly somersaulted while Miki whooped with joy. They turned twice in the air before they splashed back into the ocean. Then the filly leaped up again, this time twisting like a top. To Miki's left, she saw the shiny eel in mid leap beside them.

"Thank you!" she said to the water horse. "You rescued me!"

The filly let out a soft whinny in reply. Another image appeared in Miki's mind—the shiver shark snapping uselessly as they left it behind. The shark looked so foolish and goofy with bug eyes that Miki had to laugh.

"I didn't know horses could . . . communicate with people," Miki said, stroking the filly's soft mane. "I guess there's probably a lot I don't know about your world."

The filly nodded her head and neighed in agreement. She looked back at Miki, her eyes twinkling. Then she sent an image of Miki herself with a silly expression on her face, similar to the shiver shark's!

The water horse was *teasing* her!

"Hey!" Miki protested, but then

she joined in laughing when the filly whinnied in amusement. The eel splashed in the water nearby, obviously enjoying the joke, too.

For the rest of the day, Miki rode the coral filly around the open ocean. It was a joy to ride the filly while she surfed the crests of giant waves, sometimes dancing in the air.

When the water horse tired of leaping and flipping, she brought Miki deep under the surface, showing her a staggeringly beautiful undersea world. Miki discovered that the water horse could breathe air or water. Surprisingly, Miki felt completely comfortable breathing water herself—as long as she was in direct contact with the filly. The water horse could understand what Miki was saying underwater, too . . . although Miki's own speech sounded bubbly and funny to her own ear.

Down in the ocean depths, Miki discovered a world where wild water horses roamed free amid friendly yulung dragons and schools of glowing fish in every color. She saw huge squid shooting by with squirts of pink ink, as well as yellow seaweed wriggling like long ribbons around bubbling volcanic vents.

Miki knew she would never forget these wonders.

As the sun began to set and the filly headed back toward Awdi Salaca, Miki didn't think she'd ever felt happier.

"That was the best day I ever had! But I don't even know your name," Miki said to the water horse.

An image of Bahura Reef appeared in Miki's mind. The reddish coral of the reef gleamed in the fading sunset light. It was the same color as the filly.

"Are you telling me your name is Coral?" Miki asked.

The filly glanced back at her and then nodded, gently fluttering her long eyelashes in agreement.

Of course, Miki thought. It was the

perfect name for such a lovely creature of the sea.

After checking that no shiver sharks were near, Coral returned Miki to her canoe by the Hazard Point sea stack. Miki gave the water horse a hug around her strong neck.

"Please tell me you'll visit me again," Miki said.

Coral whinnied loudly and dipped her head in a nod.

"Thank you," Miki said softly. "I can't wait."

*M*iki's parents were amazed by the large luna pearl and the story of Coral, but they were also angry with her for going diving alone at Hazard Point.

"You know better than to go out by yourself!" Mr. Vann thundered. "Your mother was sick with worry all day. Don't disappear without telling us where you're going ever again!"

"I'm sorry," Miki said sincerely. She hadn't even considered how her adventure would affect her family. "I promise to tell you where I'm going in future."

Mr. Vann sat down at the table and held Miki's luna pearl in his hand. Its eerie glow bathed his face in silver light. "These are troubled times," he said in a softer voice. "We have to stick together."

Miki's mother applied salve to Miki's rope burns and bandaged them before sending her straight to bed.

The next morning, Miki rushed to the cove, hoping that Coral would be waiting for her.

But the filly wasn't there.

Miki slumped against a large rock and moodily tossed shells into the water. If not for her rope burns, she would have thought yesterday had been a dream.

The pearl she'd found would probably keep her family from hunger for a few weeks, but that was all. Their situation was as bleak as it had been before yesterday's adventure.

"Hey, Miki!" Lealoni called from behind her. "You coming to help clean the nets?"

"No," Miki snapped. "I don't know why we bother! Nobody catches anything in the nets anyway! Fishing is useless—our only hope is finding pearls."

Lealoni looked hurt. "Fine!" she shot back, stomping away toward the fishing area. "Don't help us! Just give up on the whole island! It's not like it's our *home* or anything!"

As the younger girl stormed away, Miki kicked a clump of sand. She knew she was being unfair—it wasn't Lealoni's fault she felt out of sorts.

After sitting for hours, watching the waves for any sign of Coral, Miki stood up and wandered aimlessly along the beach.

"Miki!" a voice called from behind her.

Wilai came sprinting around the

edge of the cove. "Have you seen . . . Lealoni?" he gasped, completely out of breath. It was strange to see him without his twin.

"No, do I look like her babysitter?" Miki asked irritably. "I haven't seen her for a couple of hours."

"No one has seen her," Wilai panted.

A shock of alarm jolted Miki. "What do you mean?" she demanded. "Didn't she show up to clean the nets?"

"No," Wilai explained. "Her parents came looking for her, but she wasn't there. Kei and Peloni are helping them search the island."

"Where could she go?" Miki wondered. "It's not that big an island!"

"I don't know," Wilai replied. "That's why I came looking for you!"

"Oh, no," Miki murmured to herself, struck with a horrible thought. "She wanted to help the island . . . and I told her fishing was useless." The story of

Miki finding the luna pearl yesterday was sure to have reached every corner of the island already.

Wilai shook his head. He was used to finishing someone else's thoughts. "No. She wouldn't go to Hazard Point . . . would she?"

Miki had the sinking feeling that, yes, Lealoni would.

Miki bolted for her canoe, but it wasn't tied to its usual tree on the beach. *Lealoni has taken it!* she realized.

Miki raced through the jungle toward Hazard Point. "Lealoni!" she screamed, when she reached the wind-swept spit of land. Scrambling over the jagged rocks, Miki stumbled toward the rocky shoreline.

She spotted Lealoni clinging to the sea stack one hundred feet offshore, ocean waves crashing around her, shooting spray skyward. The canoe had been smashed to pieces against the rocks nearby.

Miki felt sick with fear for her friend. There was no way Miki could get to the sea stack without the canoe. Lealoni would be swept into the angry ocean any moment. Unless—

"Coral, I need you!" Miki screamed. "Please help me!"

For a long, frightening moment, Miki scanned the waters and saw nothing but the crashing waves.

Then she heard a chirp beside her. The shimmering eel shimmied up on a slick rock, squealing wildly.

Coral burst through the surface of the rough surf, bobbing in the treacherous current.

"Oh, thank you for coming!" Miki gasped. She dived into the water and quickly hugged the water horse around her neck. "We need to save Lealoni. Please hurry."

Nodding, Coral carried Miki away from the shore, over the waves toward the sea stack.

Lealoni was screaming, barely hanging on as the waves relentlessly beat her against the rocks. Her mouth dropped open in shock when she saw Miki appear beside her astride the pink water horse.

"Give me your hand," Miki yelled, reaching out over the gushing water.

Lealoni's fingers closed around Miki's hand, and Miki pulled the little girl onto Coral's back.

"Watch out for the monster!" screamed Lealoni. "It's here!"

CHAPTER

6

*L*ealoni shrieked as a huge tentacle slid out of the water, grabbing at Coral.

Miki's eyes open wide, she let out a terrified scream, too.

With Miki and Lealoni on her back, Coral plunged quickly underneath the waves, deftly twirling to avoid the coiling tentacle. Then, more tentacles thrashed violently around them, trying to snag the water horse and her riders.

Lealoni held on to Miki too tightly, but the discomfort reassured Miki that

57

her friend was unhurt.

Miki saw the tentacles were connected to an enormous kraken, the biggest one she'd ever seen. It was a monstrous creature from her worst childhood nightmares, its body at least five times bigger than Coral, with sharp suckers covering its tentacles. The kraken had leathery, dark orange skin and barnacles encrusted around its huge, angry eyes.

Coral slapped the beast with her tail, right in its eye. The kraken recoiled, blinking. The water horse used the distraction to thrust herself quickly upward.

"Faster, Coral!" Miki hollered, when they reached the surface. "Get us away from here!"

Coral bolted away at top speed. It took only a few minutes for the water horse to leave the hideous kraken behind.

Between the shiver sharks and the kraken, Miki figured she knew what was keeping the fire spoops away from the reef—and the fish away from the islanders' nets!

Coral brought them safely to Awdi Salaca's fishing dock, and Miki and Lealoni climbed off the water horse onto the dock's worn planks.

"What were you thinking?" Miki demanded from Lealoni. "You could have been hurt, or—or—worse." She trembled, and grabbed Lealoni in a rough, relieved hug.

Lealoni pulled away, staring at Coral, who was bobbing alongside the dock. "She's gorgeous!" Lealoni said, hugging the water horse. "Thank you for helping Miki save me." She ran her hand along Coral's sleek scales.

Miki laughed. "Yes, Coral is the most gorgeous horse in the whole ocean."

"There they are!" Kei shouted. He had appeared with Shad on the far side of the fishing dock.

Shad turned and ran inland, returning moments later with Lealoni's parents and what seemed like the entire population of the island. Wilai had obviously raised the alarm when Miki rushed toward Hazard Point!

Lealoni's parents snatched her into a tight embrace, their faces crumpling into tears of joy that their daughter was safe.

"They saved me!" Lealoni cried. "Miki and Coral both. They saved me from the monster."

Lealoni's father narrowed his eyes. "What monster?" he asked Miki.

"The biggest kraken I've ever seen," Miki replied, shuddering. "It lives behind the reef. Its tentacles are thicker than the biggest vines on this island. It would cover half of Broad Beach."

The islanders fell quiet momentarily, but then Shad laughed, and all the islanders joined in.

"It's true!" Lealoni cried, but that

just made everyone laugh louder.

"A giant kraken!" one elder exclaimed. "I've lived on this island for almost one hundred and twenty years— you'd think we would have seen some sign of it before! Nothing that terrible lives in these waters."

"You sound just like that old water witch Mesmeera," Lealoni's mother said. "She was famous for her crazy monster stories."

"You girls just made up that story to avoid getting in trouble," Shad's father added.

"No!" Miki protested.

"We saw the monster!" Lealoni cried. "It almost ate me!"

Ignoring the girls, all the island children and some of the adults stepped toward the dock to stare at Coral. The water horse wriggled nervously backward, uneasy with all the attention.

"Can we ride her?" Peloni asked.

When Miki saw how alarmed the

water horse was becoming, she pushed through the crowd and climbed onto Coral. "Let's go," she urged the filly.

Coral slid into the sea, swimming rapidly toward the horizon.

"How rude," Miki said to Coral. "They don't believe me about the kraken, but they want to ride you." She stroked Coral gently, who made a cute little whistle sound in reply.

One thing Lealoni's mother had said stuck with Miki—the name Mesmeera. Miki had heard of the old woman, who now lived alone in a hut on a small island off the southern coast of Awdi Salaca. If the woman believed in sea monsters, maybe she would believe Miki.

"Coral, please take me to Mesmeera," Miki said.

Coral took off in the direction Miki pointed.

As Coral approached Mesmeera's island, Miki spotted an old woman sitting in a bamboo chair on a tiny dock that hung out precariously over the water. Mesmeera seemed more motherly and kind than witchy. Behind her was a tiny hut built half on a narrow spit of coral reef and half on the dock.

Mesmeera stood as Coral swam up to the dock. With surprising strength, Mesmeera helped Miki clamber onto the dock.

"Hello, my dear. What a beautiful water horse," said Mesmeera with a formal curtsy. "To what do I owe the great honor of a royal visit to my humble island?"

"Royal?" Miki asked sheepishly. "I'm just a pearl diver's daughter."

"No, not you, dear," Mesmeera said, with a broad, toothless smile. "I'm referring to this jewel of the sea." She gestured to Coral, who nickered a friendly hello.

"What do you mean by 'royal'?" asked Miki.

Mesmeera rolled her eyes. "Don't you even know who you're riding?"

Miki shook her head. "My friend Coral?"

"I believe her official title is Coral, Lady of Herd Islandar. She is a monarch of the Equinesian Seas," Mesmeera said.

Miki's mouth dropped open. She had known Coral was special, but she had never dreamed that the filly was from a royal bloodline! She glanced back at Coral, and the horse nodded her noble head gently, twitching her tail restlessly in the water.

"But you were more wrong than you realized," Mesmeera added, staring at Miki in a peculiarly curious way. "Yes, quite wrong."

"What do you mean?" Miki demanded.

"You're not simply a pearl diver's daughter. No, not at all." Mesmeera studied Miki from head to toe, walking around her, inspecting her carefully.

"You have a special destiny."

Miki was growing increasingly uncomfortable with Mesmeera's odd attentions. "My name is—"

"Miki Vann," finished Mesmeera. "Yes, I know."

"H-how?" stammered Miki.

"I'm a water sage," Mesmeera replied. "I make it my business to be aware of everything that happens in these waters, including knowing all the islanders on Awdi Salaca. Some on your island call me a witch—silly, dense-headed people. Oh, look!" the old woman cried suddenly, whirling around to face the water. "A glimmer eel!"

The eel that traveled with Coral had wriggled onto the dock and was stealing a grape from Mesmeera's bowl. Caught in the act, the eel made a funny little clicking noise that sounded like a question.

"That's all right," Mesmeera answered. "You can have it."

The eel chirped again and quickly finished the snack.

"So, Miki, I'm sure you must have a thousand questions for me," Mesmeera said.

Surprised, Miki blurted, "Yes."

"But *which* question should you ask me? Hurry, girl, ask quickly." Mesmeera snapped her fingers. She plopped back into her bamboo chair, which sagged from years of use. "I'm not some old oracle who speaks in riddles. I like to speak my mind, which is why your town elders don't want me on their island. Seems they don't like to hear the truth. But if *you* want the truth, ask away, child."

"Why didn't the fire spoops—"

"Stay?" Mesmeera finished Miki's sentence again. "An excellent question. Why *didn't* the fire spoops fertilize the reef? For starters, the reef is dying—"

"That's what Shad said!" Miki broke in.

The sage's eyes narrowed. She was obviously irritated at being interrupted. "Okay, so you already knew that the reef is dying." Mesmeera paused to pop a grape in her mouth. "But I bet you didn't know it was your fault."

7

"*My* fault?" Miki asked, shocked. "How could it be my fault? I haven't done anything to the reef!"

Mesmeera peered up at Miki, raising her gray eyebrows. "Are you a pearl diver?"

"Yes," Miki said slowly. "My family has been pearl diving for generations."

"Then you're at fault," Mesmeera said firmly. "The luna pearls are the key. Haven't you noticed how dark the waters are at night now? In years past, Bahura Reef glowed brilliantly, but now the light is flickering out."

"The luna pearls are . . . the source of the light?" Miki asked.

"Exactly." Mesmeera offered the glimmer eel a chunk of banana. He slithered up her leg, curling in Mesmeera's lap to eat the snack. Miki was surprised to see that the eel, like Coral, seemed equally comfortable breathing in the air as he did underwater.

"The luna light protects the reef, keeping predators away," Mesmeera said.

Miki reached into the pouch at her waist, feeling the warmth of the luna pearl she'd found. She pulled it out, admiring the way it shined brilliantly even in bright daylight.

Simply holding the pearl suddenly made her feel terribly guilty—now that she knew she'd stolen its light from the reef.

"I . . . *am* at fault," she murmured, stunned.

"Yes, well, at least partially," Mesmeera said. "*All* the pearl divers who take the luna pearls from the reef are at fault. I tried to explain this to your village elders years ago, but they said I was a foolish old witch. Now there are monsters in the waters; horrible beasts that lurk along our shores, scaring away the fish!"

"You know about the kraken?" Miki asked. "It almost got us earlier."

Coral nodded her head.

"Uloo," Mesmeera said, in a hushed tone. "He's a terrible creature, older than Mount Salaca. The luna pearls protected these waters from him and his kind for hundreds of years, but now that they've been harvested to near extinction, he has returned."

Miki's knees suddenly felt weak. The news was more horrible than she had imagined.

"The fire spoops won't return to the reef as long as Uloo and the shiver

sharks continue to trespass in these waters," Mesmeera said matter-of-factly. "The reef will continue to die, and the fish that live there will disappear."

"What can be done?" Miki pleaded. "I'll do anything."

Mesmeera smiled. "Uloo and the sharks need to be driven away from the reef."

Miki let out a shocked bark of laughter. "Oh, is that all?"

"That's all," Mesmeera replied. "You will find that the reef is resilient. If it is protected, it will return to its former vibrant glory."

"But what can I do?" Miki hoped Mesmeera had the answer . . . and an easy one at that.

"Why, my dear, the answer has been with you all along," Mesmeera said, pointing to the red water horse. "Why do you think Coral is here?"

Coral nodded her head excitedly, showing that she was ready to help.

"Coral?" Miki asked, surprised. "She may be royalty, but she can't possibly fight Uloo and the sharks. Not all of them."

Coral surged onto the dock, soaking Miki and Mesmeera in a sheet of water. The wooden planks creaked under her weight. The water horse trumpeted, sounding deeply offended.

The glimmer eel squealed in fright before bolting into the water.

"Never underestimate the equine," Mesmeera said, looking up at the water horse that towered over her. "They are the greatest of all creatures, with a proud history of helping humans. I suggest you apologize . . . quickly, before we get any wetter."

Miki felt ashamed. "I'm sorry to have doubted you, Coral," she told her friend sincerely.

A tickling sensation filled Miki's head as a vivid image of a gigantic oyster popped into her mind. Inside the vast oyster was the biggest luna pearl she had ever seen, glowing through the vision like a star.

Mesmeera laughed like a giddy young girl. "It is the picture-speak she sends! Do you see the pearl?"

"I see it," Miki replied. "What does it mean?"

"Coral is giving you your answer," Mesmeera explained. "The horses of Celestial Deep have a great luna pearl— the Heart of the Sea—in their possession. This giant, magical pearl has the ability to protect Bahura Reef. You must go immediately—"

"But," Miki interrupted, feeling dazed, "but the Heart of the Sea is a myth, isn't it?"

Coral neighed loudly, confirming Mesmeera's story.

Miki closed her eyes for a long moment. She was dealing with legendary forces now . . . a giant magical pearl, a vicious kraken, and a royal water horse.

But she had never backed down from a challenge in her life.

Slowly, Miki looked up into the eyes of the royal water horse. "Coral, can you take me to this pearl?"

The filly slid off the dock into the water, lining up her back with the dock so Miki could mount.

"It seems you have your answer," Mesmeera said softly. "I envy you, Miki Vann. Sadly, I am too old for such adventures."

"Thank you, Mesmeera." Miki kissed the old woman on her rough cheek. "You'll see. The reef will be healed. I'll bring the pearl back as quick as I can."

"I know you will, dear," Mesmeera said. "Before you go, I have one more word of warning. The Heart of the Sea is unlike anything you've ever seen. It has a guardian, a horse protector named Mahina. To get this pearl you will need more than just your diving knife. You will need to be true to yourself and hon-est above all else. The oyster's guardian will sense any deceit."

Miki nodded. "Will you do me a favor?" she asked the elder. "Would you send my parents a message about what I'm doing and how important it is? They'll worry anyway, but at least they'll know I'm with Coral."

"I'd be honored," Mesmeera replied. "Good luck to you, Miki Vann."

8

Miki's fingers trembled with nervous excitement as she climbed onto Coral's back. The water horse and Miki slid under the waves, followed by the glimmer eel. His cheeks were filled with grapes.

Miki still couldn't believe she didn't need to hold her breath as long as she was riding Coral. It was a bizarre sensation.

But it was a good thing they didn't have to stop every few minutes for Miki to breathe, since the trip took a lot longer than Miki had expected.

During the first afternoon, Coral pulled up alongside a pod of dolphins. Miki cheered in delight as Coral flipped out of the water in sync with them.

"I'll bet you can outflip them!" Miki shouted to Coral, who was only too happy to take up the challenge. The playful animals were very agile and gave the water horse stiff competition, soaring and twirling in the air. Each time one of the dolphins performed an amazing maneuver, the others cheered.

But finally Coral neighed loudly and, with a mighty flip of her tail, launched herself high up out of the water. She seemed to hang in the sunny sky, slowly looping her body around completely three times. Then Coral slipped without a splash back into the sea.

When Coral surfaced, Miki shouted in triumph and the dolphins smacked the water with their fins in admiration.

Coral and Miki continued their

journey, traveling by skimming along just below the waves. They only occasionally surfaced to get a look around. Coral stopped for the night beside a small, deserted isle, so Miki could rest on land and drink fresh water.

In the morning, they headed back out to sea as soon as the sun rose. The trip was fun and scary at the same time. Miki had never been so far away from home nor for so long. She'd never even spent the night on one of the neighboring islands of the Equinesian archipelago!

The second afternoon, a violent squall broke overhead, and Coral had to dive deep to avoid the turbulence of the choppy, storm-shaken ocean. They traveled deep all through the night, and Miki slept clinging to Coral's neck.

When the storm passed the next day, Coral surfaced near a fast schooner headed toward the mainland of North of North. The sailors tossed food down to Miki—bread and cheese and salty meat.

That evening, Miki spotted two winged horses flying through the clouds overhead, lit up in pastel colors by the setting sun. It was the first time Miki had seen flying horses. Before meeting Coral, she would have been astonished. But after all the amazing things she'd seen in the last few days, the lovely winged creatures seemed almost commonplace.

As they traveled farther and farther, Miki realized the world of North of North was larger and more exotic than she had ever expected—far more impressive even than the way it was described in the stories the elders told.

After four long days, Coral and Miki finally approached the undersea kingdom of Celestial Deep.

From a distance, the kingdom looked like a monumental coral reef. But as they got closer, Miki could see that Celestial Deep was a vast, magnificent city. It was a series of living structures created out of coral and layers of seaweed and undersea plants. The city had obviously been grown, rather than built, over the course of many centuries. Volcanic vents in the ocean floor bubbled around the perimeter of the city, providing heat, nutrients, and oxygen-rich water.

The ocean around the city was teeming with an astonishing variety of deep-sea life. Sea anemones, sea fans, seaweed, and a thick, dark blue grass called sweetwater covered the seabed around the city and its avenues like a lush lawn gently swaying in the ebb and flow of the current. Sea creatures that Miki had never imagined—flippered camels and tiny blue spiders that traveled in bubbles—swam about, busy with their daily lives.

Luna pearls had been placed along the paths that weaved through the city, bathing everything in soft light.

Miki was astounded by Celestial Deep, but most of all she was surprised by the number of water horses who lived

there. They crowded around the undersea stables, gathered in open meeting squares, and raced through the avenues.

Coral carried Miki along causeways, past submerged stone jetties, zipping in and out through gardens of seaweed and kelp forests.

Finally, Coral arrived at a wide boulevard leading to the magnificent Islandar Castle. The castle's looming narrow spires towered above the city, each one looking like the horn of a gigantic unicorn. As Miki stared up at them, the spires seemed to waver in the ripples and eddies of water circulating around them.

Armored water horses rushed over to flank Coral. Two guards led the way as they approached the castle. Trumpetfish blared their horns as Coral and Miki were ushered through glistening gates into a sandy courtyard.

A fussy-looking parrotfish wearing spectacles blocked Coral's entrance. "Lady Coral, where have you *been*?" he squawked. Miki was pleased to discover she could understand the fat parrotfish. Its voice sounded strange, though—screechy and gurgling at the same time. "You're completely off your schedule! It will take weeks of hard work to get back on track," the parrotfish whined.

Coral reared up and zoomed around him into the castle's interior. It was the first time Miki had ever seen her friend appear frightened. They quickly lost the parrotfish in the maze of corridors that wound through the castle.

At last, Coral and Miki came to a vast sliding door that opened onto a grand imperial hall. The domed space was crowded with water horse dignitaries and other water creatures representing their domains. All the undersea animals hushed as Miki and Coral approached the dais in the center of the chamber.

An extremely handsome water horse hovered in the water in front of two empty raised platforms. He glared at

Miki and a series of rapid images flickered through her mind, but they were too fast for her to figure out what he was telling her.

"I'm sorry," Miki said. "But I don't understand. Maybe if you send the images more slowly?"

The noble water horse breathed out a stream of bubbles in frustration. Then he sent out a very strong image of the parrotfish.

In moments, the parrotfish zoomed into the chamber, zipping over to the official. He gave Coral a quick glare before turning toward Miki. "My name is Polyo," the parrotfish told her in his odd gurgling squawk. "I am the Royal Herald of Herd Islandar, and I will translate for Councilor Echevar."

Miki sighed with relief. "Thank you," she said.

Another barrage of images from Councilor Echevar flooded Miki's mind. Polyo paused for a moment, and then translated. "Councilor Echevar welcomes the return of Lady Coral," the parrotfish said. "But he doesn't understand why a human would come uninvited to Celestial Deep, especially a small child. Please state your business quickly and clearly, so that we may judge your worthiness to stand before us."

Coral nickered softly, encouraging Miki to speak up.

"Um, all right," Miki replied. She felt very nervous to be addressing the whole royal court. "I'm from the island of Awdi Salaca," she blurted. "We're in deep trouble. I've come to beg you to help us."

Councilor Echevar raised his muzzle higher in the water, sending out more flickering images.

"And why should we?" Polyo translated.

"The luna pearls are almost all gone," Miki explained, "and Bahura Reef has been invaded. Uloo, a vicious giant kraken, is killing and eating the fish. Shiver sharks are everywhere, scaring away the fire spoops." Miki paused as all the emotions of the past few days welled up and threatened to overwhelm her.

Coral whinnied loudly, as though emphasizing Miki's words.

This time Councilor Echevar sent an image Miki understood—a handsome water horse, turning his back on her.

"How is this our problem?" interpreted the parrotfish.

"The reef is dying!" Miki cried.

*C*ouncilor Echevar paused for a long moment and then swished his tail through the water before he replied.

"That is truly tragic," Polyo translated. "But he is told that your island's people are to blame. They took too many of the pearls from the waters, and now that their protective light is gone, you come seeking help." The herald's voice was stern. "How is your carelessness any concern of ours? What would you have us do?"

Miki felt the eyes of everyone in

the court fixed on her. Coral nuzzled Miki's arm, giving her the courage to continue.

"A water sage named Mesmeera told me you have a giant pearl that could protect our reef so it can heal," Miki said to Councilor Echevar.

Rearing up in surprise, Councilor Echevar let out a loud neigh and blasted the court with frenzied images.

Polyo swam in a tight circle before he translated. "She means the Heart of the Sea!" he exclaimed. "Dear girl, the Heart of the Sea is our national treasure. We will not be giving *that* away today!"

"Please," Miki begged. "You must help us."

Councilor Echevar snorted bubbles again and turned his head rudely away from Miki.

"'Must'?" interpreted the parrotfish. "Child, we have been courteous because you entered these halls with Lady Coral, but we are under no obligation to help you."

Miki tightened her hands to fists. She was frustrated and furious with the councilor. "Our island's pearls light all the rooms in this castle!" she argued hotly.

Councilor Echevar glared witheringly at Miki.

"The light from our Heart of the Sea will never leave Celestial Deep," Polyo translated.

Coral trumpeted, a shocking burst of noise that took everyone by surprise. Miki had to hold on tightly as Coral thrust herself onto the dais.

Coral used vivid images to explain that the king and queen of Celestial Deep had sent her to investigate what was causing Bahura Reef to weaken. Now she had returned and demanded that the court respect her findings. Miki was impressed by how much easier it was to understand her friend than the flickering thoughts of Echevar.

The councilor stepped back, intimidated by Coral's intense emotion. But he quickly controlled himself and replied.

"We acknowledge Lady Coral's contribution," Polyo translated. "But her opinions do not sway our judgment. By order of the king, Councilor Echevar has authority over all issues brought before this court."

Something had been bothering Miki since her encounter with Mesmeera. The water sage had a great understanding of the sea, and she had sent Miki here for a reason. Miki was just beginning to understand what that reason might be.

"Your Heart of the Sea comes from Bahura Reef. It was given to you as a gift of friendship between our peoples." Miki continued, "It was meant to protect you in your hour of need. What kind of creatures are you that you won't now help us? If you have any honor, you'll return it to us."

The royal hall erupted in shocked

whinnies from the court.

Councilor Echevar flicked his long tail, his eyes blazing at Miki.

"You can't be serious," interpreted Polyo.

"I am," Miki replied. "To you, the pearl is now just a beautiful treasure. But to us in Awdi Salaca, it will bring back life to our reef. I humbly ask you to do what's right."

The councilor neighed, and was about to reply, when fanfare blared from the entrance to the chamber.

Polyo puffed up his fat body. "Announcing His and Her Majesty, King Treasure and Queen Edana," he squawked. "Kind, honorable, and wise rulers of Celestial Deep and the watery wonders around it!"

Miki gasped as two of the most beautiful water horses she'd ever seen swept into the room. The female was the same red color as Coral, but her mane was bigger and wilder. The queen's tail

didn't end in a flipper, but in delicate, fiery trailing tendrils. King Treasure was smaller than his consort, with a red body and a sharp horn growing out of his head that was the same shape as Celestial Deep's pointed spires. The king's short mane was bright orange. The monarchs took their positions hovering in the water above their royal platforms in the center of the chamber.

With a deep bow, Councilor Echevar backed away to join the courtiers on the side of the chamber.

Queen Edana nodded her head. The silver tiara that adorned her forehead twinkled with dozens of tiny luna pearls. She flashed quick images to the court.

"The queen will handle this situation, if the king doesn't mind," Polyo translated.

King Treasure replied, and the parrotfish said aloud, "Yes, dear."

"You are from Awdi Salaca?" the

queen asked Miki, interpreted by Polyo. "The queen has wanted to visit your island. She hears it's the crown jewel of the Equinesian Seas."

Miki noticed the glimmer eel twined around the queen's foreleg. The eel chirped cheerfully at her, and Miki smiled at him.

"Spark, my little friend here, has told me everything, although I suspect he's a bit biased," Queen Edana explained. "He's quite smitten with you, and Spark has a tendency to exaggerate when he's excited."

Stunned, Miki simply blinked at the queen. "Hello, ma'am." Miki bowed awkwardly. "My name is Miki."

Queen Edana sent more images, and Polyo said, "So the queen has heard that you're in need of the Heart of the Sea—"

Spark hissed something into Queen Edana's ear.

The queen nodded to the eel

before addressing the whole court. "We should help our neighbors," she explained through Polyo. "We are all stewards of the sea, are we not?"

The queen glared at Councilor Echevar, who seemed for a moment as though he might argue. But then he stepped back and bowed meekly.

"Yes," Polyo translated for Queen Edana, "that's what I thought."

Coral nickered softly, and Queen Edana faced her.

"The queen's niece, Lady Coral, has made a request," interpreted Polyo, "and our queen grants her the opportunity to oversee the transportation of the Heart of the Sea to Bahura Reef, its new home."

Miki buried her face into Coral's mane, not wanting the monarchs nor the rest of the court to see her crying in joyful relief.

10

*C*oral made arrangements for the trip, helped by the royal staff of hundreds of horses and other sea creatures. The Heart of the Sea would be taken to Awdi Salaca, where it would be positioned in a new place of honor on the reef.

It would take a couple of days to prepare for the journey, so Miki was given a private chamber in the castle.

The first night, Miki had trouble falling asleep. It was the only time since she'd left on her adventure that she felt really homesick. The bed of soft seaweed was very comfortable, but Miki longed for her familiar hammock with the ocean breezes wafting through the open windows of her parents' house.

The next day, after lunch, Miki, Coral, and Spark went out for a ride so Coral could show Miki more of Celestial Deep.

As the afternoon became evening, Coral carried Miki into a small, carefully tended garden. Many species of lovely ocean plants grew along the garden's coral colonnades and archways. As Miki gazed at the beauty of the simple garden, a vision sent from Coral formed in her mind.

The image was of Miki holding a delicate oyster—a species she had never seen before. Coral blew bubbles in excitement and nodded her head for Miki to turn around.

In a sandy corner of the garden, Miki noticed oysters just like the image

Coral had showed her. Spark gathered one of the shells and brought it to Miki. Coral trumpeted and nickered—she wanted Miki to have it.

"Thank you, Coral."

It took only a simple stroke of Miki's knife to cut open the oyster. Tears welled up in Miki's eyes when she saw what was inside.

It was a perfectly formed golden pearl.

Miki threw her arms around Coral and Spark. "Oh, thank you," she gushed. "It's the most wonderful gift I've ever gotten!"

The next morning, the procession was finally ready to depart for the long journey. King Treasure and Queen Edana led the party. Miki followed on Coral. Behind them were the royal court and more regal equines. The Heart of the Sea, in its ornate oyster shell, was ferried by four large water horses at the end of the procession.

Miki was briefly introduced to Mahina, the pearl's guardian. The petite water horse took her job very seriously. Darting back and forth, she never let anyone, including the royal family, approach within ten feet of the Heart of the Sea.

"Mahina's very beautiful," Miki said to Coral, "but she seems a little . . . well, *small* to be the guardian of such a large pearl."

Coral whinnied in laughter, and shook her head.

The trip back to Awdi Salaca was slower than the journey to Celestial Deep had been. But that was all right with Miki, since it gave her the chance to spend quality time with Coral. They took any opportunity to escape the procession and explore the ocean on their own or with Spark. Together they discovered a deep cavern filled with humming crystals and met a pod of whales, including the most adorable newborn whale calf. They played tag with a group of young, boisterous yulung dragons, which reminded Miki of Shad, somehow.

It took nearly a week for the procession to approach Bahura Reef. They reached it on a clear evening, with the moons just poking through a few scattered clouds.

Polyo had been sent ahead to Awdi Salaca to prepare the way for the king and queen of Celestial Deep. Miki couldn't imagine how the islanders would react to receiving a royal message from a talking fish!

When Awdi Salaca finally came into view, Miki was surprised by how small the island seemed.

But she couldn't wait to get home.

CHAPTER

11

𝒜s the procession came around the reef toward Broad Beach, Miki saw that all the islanders were waiting in their canoes offshore.

The royal family broke away from the rest of the procession as they entered the bay, leaving behind their entourage with the great luna pearl in the deeper waters. The island's elders welcomed the king and queen warmly with gifts of flower garlands.

Miki tried hard not to burst into tears when she saw her family waving from their canoe. Coral carried her swiftly over to them. Miki couldn't stop her tears from flowing freely once she had climbed into their canoe and was enveloped in the embrace of her parents and brother. When Miki finally pulled away, she saw Lealoni with her family in a nearby boat. Waving to her best friend, fresh tears rolled down Miki's cheeks.

Finally, the time had come for the Heart of the Sea to be presented.

King Treasure neighed loudly, commanding the four stallions to bring forth the giant oyster. The water horses sped across the water, the massive oyster skimming behind with little Mahina perched on the edge.

Miki cheered along with all the islanders as the oyster holding the pearl that would save them was transported into place beside the reef.

On the king's signal, Mahina leaped off the oyster and released it from its tethers. With a tremendous gurgle of churning water, the oyster sank.

"Look!" Lealoni shrieked. "The monster!"

The islanders' cheers turned to screams as a thick, sucker-covered tentacle rose out of the water and splashed down after the oyster. Guards rushed the royal family from the reef.

"It's Uloo," Miki whispered, trying to stifle the flickers of fear that were threatening to freeze her. She jumped off the canoe onto Coral's back. "We've got to protect that pearl," she said grimly. "Let's go."

With a loud neigh, Coral dived under the surface, racing toward the monstrous kraken. Spark streaked over to them, flashing in excitement as they all sped toward the spot where the giant oyster rested on a coral platform on the reef. In front of the oyster, little Mahina was already facing down the tentacled invader.

As Miki, Coral, and Spark got

close to Mahina, the guardian's eyes widened in alarm. She trumpeted a warning for them to stay back.

"But we want to help you!" Miki cried. "I want to protect my island!"

Mahina dodged one of Uloo's grasping tentacles and then used her flipper tail to swish sand into the kraken's eyes, blinding him momentarily. The little water horse zipped over to Miki, staring right into her eyes.

Miki was surprised to find her mind opening up under Mahina's brilliant gaze. Mahina began reading Miki's thoughts.

Mesmeera had said that Miki would need to be true to herself and completely honest to gain Mahina's trust. So she opened herself up and let the guardian have full access to everything in her mind. The sensation was strangely itchy.

Miki felt proud as Mahina saw images of her rescuing Lealoni from Uloo, befriending Coral and Spark, meeting with Mesmeera, and standing up to Councilor Echevar. But then Miki felt embarrassed when Mahina inspected images of her disobeying her parents to dive for oysters at Hazard Point and snapping at Lealoni on the beach.

Finally, Mahina dug deeper into Miki's heart. There she saw Miki's true connection with Coral, her endless love for Awdi Salaca, and her genuine desire to protect and heal the island she adored.

Mahina pulled her attention away from Miki just as Uloo swung his tentacles around for another attack. As Mahina slipped through the kraken's grasp, she sent Miki a final vision—a scene of Miki, Coral, and Spark opening the oyster while Mahina fended off the kraken.

Miki nodded, and Coral wasted no time carrying her down to the massive oyster. Holding her breath, Miki quickly dismounted. She wondered how she could open such an enormous shell.

Her little oyster knife wasn't going to work!

Miki could feel the pulsing life of the massive creature in its shell, and it occurred to her that the Heart of the Sea was a *living being*.

Maybe instead of forcing the shell open, she thought, *I should* talk *to the Heart of the Sea*.

"Can you hear me?" she asked the huge oyster, feeling a little foolish as she knocked gently on its shell. "My name is Miki Vann, and we need your help." Speaking caused her to lose some air, but she had a strong feeling that talking was the only way.

Before she could say anything more, a rush of water turbulence made Miki look up. Uloo had swooped close to the oyster and was stretching out two tentacles to grab it. Miki let out a little scream as she ducked under a tentacle. Coral and Spark also dived to avoid the attack.

Then Mahina inserted herself between Uloo and the oyster. Just as the kraken was about to grab the little guardian, Mahina suddenly flickered—and began to duplicate. In seconds, there were ten ferocious little Mahinas protecting the Heart of the Sea! All the Mahinas kicked their forelegs, forcing Uloo back against the reef.

Uloo made a strange, piercing call that echoed underwater and hurt Miki's ears.

A second later, two big, nasty-looking shiver sharks appeared, slicing through the water toward Coral and Miki.

Mahina was too busy keeping Uloo at bay to help. With a brave whinny, Coral reared up in front of the sharks, boxing them back. Spark zipped between the sharks, distracting them with his shimmer.

Miki kneeled down on the oyster.

Her lungs were tightening. She had to get it open now!

"Please," she begged the Heart of the Sea. "I am from the island of Awdi Salaca. We brought you back here to Bahura Reef to protect our waters from terrible monsters. You are the only one who can help us. I beg you, mighty one, open your shell and share your light."

Miki felt the oyster lurch inside the shell, but it didn't open.

"Please," Miki tried again, feeling desperate as she grew light-headed. She knew Coral, Spark, and Mahina couldn't hold off the creatures forever. "Please, open your shell and shine your light. I promise . . . I promise . . ."

But what did Miki really have to promise?

Suddenly, she knew what she could offer.

"I promise," Miki said firmly, "that the islanders of Awdi Salaca will harvest luna pearls . . . with your permission only.

We will respect the oysters, we will respect the reef, and we will respect all creatures of the ocean as we respect ourselves. I swear this to you, Heart of the Sea."

The oyster rumbled under her feet and slowly lifted its lid.

Miki trod water above the massive shell as little streams of bright light became visible. As the oyster opened even wider, the light increased in intensity until blinding silvery beams of brilliance burst forth.

Miki shielded her eyes with her hands, turning away from the wonderful radiance.

The splendor of the Heart of the Sea illuminated the whole area, bringing Bahura Reef to a full, glorious glow.

Miki saw the shiver sharks shying away from the light, and they quickly retreated from Spark and Coral. Coral snorted in defiance after the escaping sharks.

Uloo screeched, waving its giant

tentacles, scorched by the light. In a final attack, it jetted its body under all the battling Mahinas and swooped up suddenly at the open oyster, raising its extended abdomen.

Miki guessed what Uloo might do. She held on to her last bit of breath and dived down into the oyster. Closing her eyes against the glare, Miki wrapped her body around the giant pearl.

The kraken squirted a cloud of thick, black ink out of its mantle, trying to coat the pearl and extinguish its light.

But Uloo managed only to dye Miki's back.

When the ink cleared, Miki swam out of the oyster, releasing the full blast of its illumination into Uloo's eyes.

Uloo screeched again, but the light from the Heart of the Sea was too powerful. The hideous kraken retreated, twisting and shaking violently.

At last, Uloo fled, slinking off into the vast darkness of the ocean depths.

CHAPTER

12

*C*oral swam over and Miki hopped onto her friend's back. The burning breathlessness in Miki's lungs eased instantly. Miki couldn't stop grinning—she knew this was the beginning of a new life for Bahura Reef.

Mahina made sure the Heart of the Sea was safely positioned on the coral cradle that would be its new home. The light from the great luna pearl was already warming the reef, encouraging the small sea creatures from their hiding spots. It would take a long time for the reef to heal fully, but at least it would not come to anymore harm.

From Coral's back, Miki bowed to the Heart of the Sea. "Thank you, mighty one," she said to the oyster. "Your generosity will live on forever in our legends, and we will keep our promise for as long as you keep our waters safe from harm."

Then Coral carried Miki to the surface. As they broke into the open air, a roar of cheers and applause exploded from the islanders on their canoes.

Miki waved shyly, overcome by the attention. She wanted nothing more than to return to the warm embrace of her family and friends, but before Miki could join the celebration, there was one person she had to visit first.

"Coral," she whispered into her friend's ear, "please take me to Mesmeera."

The water sage was waiting for Miki at the end of her rickety dock.

"We did it!" squealed Miki, jumping onto the dock. Coral trumpeted excitedly, and Spark joyfully flipped in the air.

"Of course you did," Mesmeera replied. "I never doubted you. Although I didn't expect you to return half stained with kraken ink! But don't worry, it will wash off in the sea after a few days."

Miki laughed and hugged the old woman. "The village elders now know that you were right," she told Mesmeera. "You can come visit me now instead of hiding on your island."

Mesmeera arched an eyebrow. "I like my island," she answered.

"I know you do," Miki said with a giggle. "Well, then, Coral and I will come and visit *you*. Often."

Spark smacked his glittering tail down on the water.

"Oh, and Spark, too, of course," Miki added. "Just as long as you keep giving him grapes!"

Mesmeera laughed. "You'd better get back to your family," she told Miki. "I know they've missed you."

"All right," Miki said, "but before I go, I want to show you something." She quickly untied her pouch and pulled out the small golden pearl Coral had given her.

Mesmeera gaped with amazement. "That is a truly royal gift," she said.

"I know," Miki replied, beaming. "Isn't it wonderful?"

Mesmeera peered at the pearl more closely. "May I?" she asked. When Miki nodded, Mesmeera took the pearl, holding it carefully in her palm. "This is more than just a rare golden pearl . . . much more."

"What is it?" asked Miki, the smile fading from her face.

"This is a drop of golden essence," Mesmeera replied, her voice an awed whisper. The water sage locked her gaze on Coral. "The energy contained in this single pearl will bring life to anything, won't it?"

Coral nodded solemnly, her eyes shining.

A vision of a vibrant Bahura Reef teeming with abundant life appeared in Miki's mind. With the golden pearl, Miki could instantly heal the reef completely.

Her mission was not yet complete.

After quickly saying good-bye to Mesmeera, Miki, Coral, and Spark hurried back to Awdi Salaca.

As soon as they reached the shore of Broad Beach, the islanders swarmed around Miki.

"There's one more thing I have to do!" she shouted over the noise of the excited homecoming. "Come on, everyone! Follow me!"

When Miki reached the corner of the beach, she started up the steep path toward Silver Rock, and all the islanders climbed up with her. Lealoni hurried forward and slipped her hand into Miki's, who squeezed it gratefully.

Finally, Miki reached the grassy outcropping sixty feet above the aquamarine ocean. Far below, she could see Coral swimming in the surf beside Queen Edana, King Treasure, and Mahina. Behind them, Bahura Reef glowed brightly with the light of the protective Heart of the Sea.

When all the islanders had gathered around her at Silver Rock, Miki pulled Coral's gift from her waist pouch. The golden pearl twinkled softly in her hand.

Miki closed her eyes for a moment, hoping this gift to the sea would bring the fire spoops back to the reef and new life back to Awdi Salaca.

"I give this gift to my people," Miki called out in a strong voice, "so that we may live in harmony with the Equinesian Seas for now and forever." She raised the golden pearl above her head.

The pearl burst. Golden drops of healing essence dripped down Miki's hand, and magical, liquid gold seeped through her fingers.

"Thank you, Coral," Miki whispered.

And she dived.

Go to
www.bellasara.com
and enter the webcode below.
Enjoy!

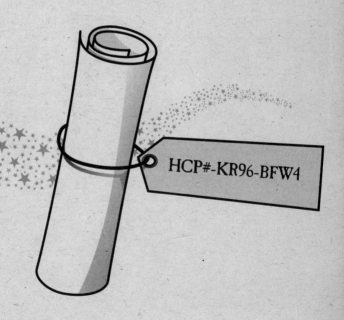

HCP#-KR96-BFW4